DINOSAUR PROFILES

TRICERATOPS

Titles in the Dinosaur Profiles series include:

Brachiosaurus

Caudipteryx

Deinonychus

Edmontosaurus

Scipionyx

Stegosaurus

Triceratops

Tyrannosaurus

DINOSAUR PROFILES

TRICERATOPS

Text by Fabio Marco Dalla Vecchia
Illustrations by Leonello Calvetti and Luca Massini

BLACKBIRCH®
PRESS

THOMSON
GALE

San Diego • Detroit • New York • San Francisco • Cleveland • New Haven, Conn. • Waterville, Maine • London • Munich

THOMSON

GALE

For more information, contact
The Gale Group, Inc.
27500 Drake Rd.
Farmington Hills, MI 48331-3535
Or you can visit our Internet site at http://www.gale.com

Computer illustrations 3D and 2D: Leonello Calvetti and Luca Massini

Photographs: pages 22–23 Louie Psihoyos/Grazia Neri

LIBRARY OF CONGRESS CATALOGING-IN-PUBLICATION DATA

Dalla Vecchia, Fabio Marco.
 Triceratops / text by Fabio Marco Dalla Vecchia; illustrations by Leonello Calvetti and Luca Massini.
  p. cm. — (Dinosaur profiles)
 Includes bibliographical references and index.
 ISBN 1-4103-0494-9 (paperback : alk. paper)
 ISBN 1-4103-0331-4 (hardback : alk. paper)
 1. Triceratops—Juvenile literature. I. Calvetti, Leonello. II. Massini, Luca. III. Title. IV. Series: Dalla Vecchia, Fabio Marco. Dinosaur profiles.

 QE862.O65D38 2004
 567.915'8—dc22   2004008700

Printed in China
10 9 8 7 6 5 4 3 2 1

Contents

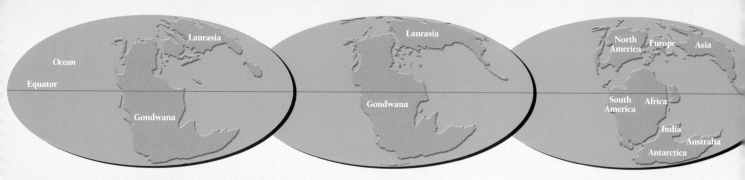

Late Triassic	Early Jurassic	Middle Jurassic
227–206 million years ago	206–176 million years ago	176–159 million years ago

A Changing World

Earth's long history began 4.6 billion years ago. Dinosaurs are some of the most fascinating animals from the planet's long past.

The word *dinosaur* comes from the word *dinosauria*. This word was invented by the English scientist Richard Owen in 1842. It comes from two Greek words, *deinos* and *sauros*. Together, these words mean "terrifying lizards."

The dinosaur era, also called the Mesozoic era, lasted from 248 million years ago to 65 million years ago. It is divided into three periods. The first, the Triassic period, lasted 42 million years. The second, the Jurassic period, lasted 61 million years. The third, the Cretaceous period, lasted 79 million years. Dinosaurs ruled the world for a huge time span of 160 million years.

Like dinosaurs, mammals appeared at the end of the Triassic period. During the time of dinosaurs, mammals were small animals the size of a mouse. Only after dinosaurs became extinct did mammals develop into the many forms that exist

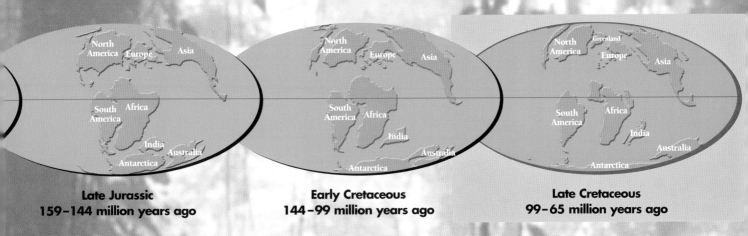

Late Jurassic
159–144 million years ago

Early Cretaceous
144–99 million years ago

Late Cretaceous
99–65 million years ago

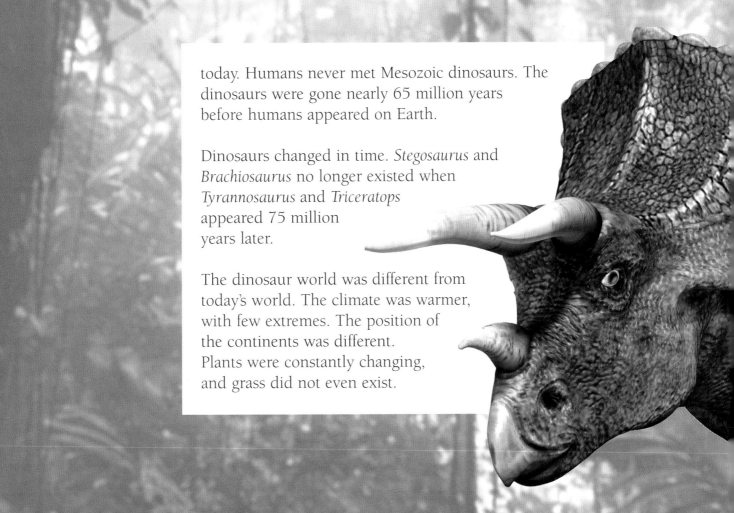

today. Humans never met Mesozoic dinosaurs. The dinosaurs were gone nearly 65 million years before humans appeared on Earth.

Dinosaurs changed in time. *Stegosaurus* and *Brachiosaurus* no longer existed when *Tyrannosaurus* and *Triceratops* appeared 75 million years later.

The dinosaur world was different from today's world. The climate was warmer, with few extremes. The position of the continents was different. Plants were constantly changing, and grass did not even exist.

A HORNED GIANT

Triceratops belonged to the Ceratopsidae family, or ceratopsids. Ceratopsids are known as "horned dinosaurs" because of the horns on their heads. *Triceratops* had a long horn above each eye. There was a much shorter one on the tip of the snout. The short horn made *Triceratops* look like a huge rhinoceros. *Triceratops* also had a large nostril, and its snout was hooked like a parrot's beak. Above its head and neck was a wide, bony frill, like a giant collar. The frill had small bony lumps along the edge. It has been suggested that the frill helped give off excess heat when the animal's body temperature got too high. Elephants do the same thing when they flap their large ears.

The only parts of *Triceratops* horns that have ever been found as fossils are the bony cores. They are up to 35 inches (90 cm) long. On the living *Triceratops*, the core had a covering that made it much bigger.

Triceratops was 20 to 28 feet (6 to 8 m) long and up to 13 feet (4 m) tall. Its large, stocky body was supported by four sturdy legs. Its tail and neck were short, but the head was large compared to the rest of its body. It was more than 6 feet (2 m) long and was held up by powerful muscles. An adult *Triceratops* weighed between 5.5 and 6.6 tons (5 and 6 metric tons), as much as a large elephant. Like most large animals, *Triceratops* probably could not move easily or quickly. *Triceratops* lived in North America about 65 million years ago at the end of the Cretaceous period of the Mesozoic era. Fossils have been found in Alberta and Saskatchewan in Canada. They have also been found in Montana, North Dakota, South Dakota, Wyoming, and Colorado.

Triceratops was one of the last dinosaurs to live on Earth. Its bones have been found just a few yards below the level in the rock that scientists think marks the end of the dinosaur era.

NORTH

AMERICA

This map shows North America as it was in the Late Cretaceous period. The dark brown patches indicate mountains. The red dots indicate *Triceratops* fossil discovery sites.

TRICERATOPS BABIES

Triceratops mothers laid large round eggs in nests in the sand. They were too large to sit on the eggs as birds do. This meant that both the hatchlings and the eggs needed protection from predators. The adults of the herd probably watched over the nests.

Triceratops hatchlings had very large heads, wide eyes, and small bumps where the horns would later grow. These bumps would eventually become dangerous weapons. However, during the first months of its life, a *Triceratops* baby was helpless.

HERDS

Triceratops lived in herds. The herds wandered along the coastal plains of North America looking for plants to eat. In those days, the region was covered by a semitropical forest. There were also many rivers and lakes.

A young *Triceratops* stayed close to
the herd so it would not become prey
to a *Tyrannosaurus*, the largest predator of
the time. When looking for food or water
in the forest, a young *Triceratops* would not
wander far from the adults.

Duels

Triceratops was a plant eater, but it was very big and could defend itself. During breeding season, males fought battles to win mates. Their large skulls could withstand the force of two heads butting together.

Triceratops's bony frill made them look bigger to their opponents. It also protected their necks when two opponents locked their long horns.

Defense

More dangerous than fights for mates were large meat-eating dinosaurs, especially *Tyrannosaurus*. Some adult *Triceratops* fossils have holes made by the teeth of these predators. This shows that *Tyrannosaurus* either attacked *Triceratops* or ate the remains of dead ones. *Tyrannosaurus* was probably the only dinosaur that would dare to attack an adult *Triceratops*. Young dinosaurs were easier prey, however. The adult *Triceratops* would form a defensive circle to protect the young ones when a predator attacked.

THE TRICERATOPS BODY

Even though *Triceratops* was large, it had a small brain. It had a strong sense of smell, however.

Its teeth were in the back of its mouth. They were unusually shaped, with a small cutting surface and a large, two-branched root. When *Triceratops* closed its mouth, its rows of teeth worked like the blades of a pair of scissors. They could cut through even the toughest plant material.

Its legs were strong and stubby to support its huge body. The front feet had five toes, and the back feet had four. They left unique footprints that have only rarely been found in fossil form.

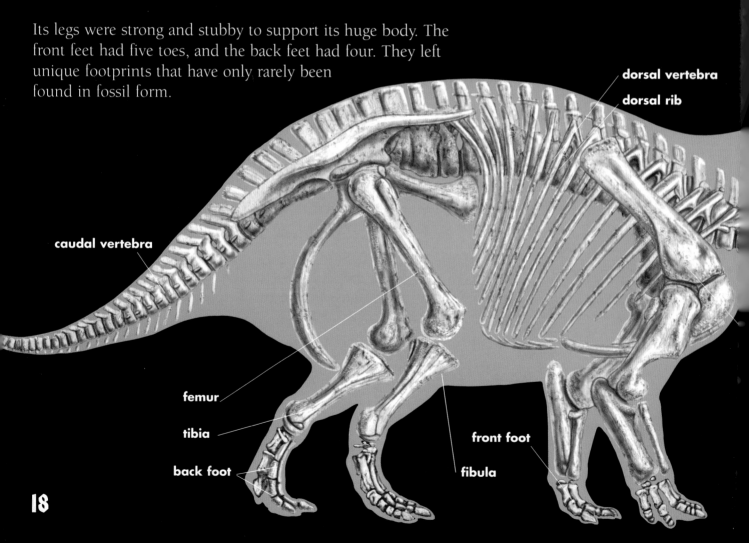

dorsal vertebra

dorsal rib

caudal vertebra

femur

tibia

back foot

front foot

fibula

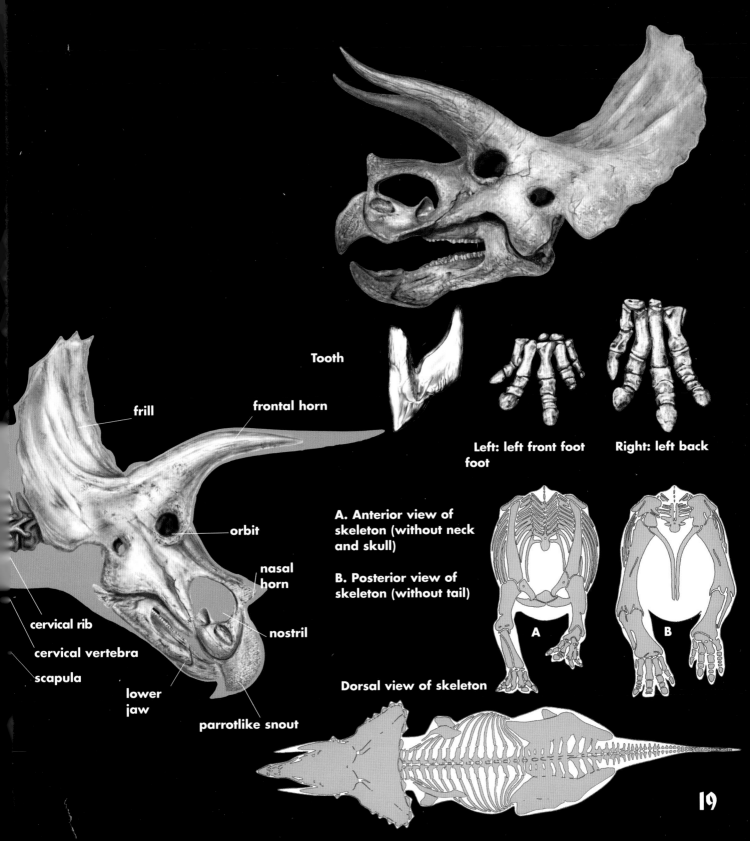

Tooth

frill

frontal horn

orbit

nasal
horn

nostril

cervical rib

cervical vertebra

scapula

lower
jaw

parrotlike snout

Left: left front foot
foot

Right: left back

A. Anterior view of
skeleton (without neck
and skull)

B. Posterior view of
skeleton (without tail)

Dorsal view of skeleton

19

DIGGING UP TRICERATOPS

The first *Triceratops* fossils found were two long horn cores. They were discovered in 1887 near Denver, Colorado. American pale-ontologist Charles O. Marsh said they were just buffalo horns.

In 1889, however, dinosaur hunter John Bell Hatcher found a nearly complete *Triceratops* skull in Wyoming. Marsh then realized his mistake and named the dinosaur *Triceratops*. This name came from the Greek words meaning "face with three horns." Over the next few years, Hatcher dug up more than forty *Triceratops* skulls and bones.

Triceratops is the most common dinosaur found. At least fifty nearly complete skulls and many other bones from both adult and young dinosaurs have been collected. Most *Triceratops* fossils are skulls. It was not until 1994 that two partial skeletons were dug up in North Dakota. They were nicknamed Willy and Raymond. There are original skulls or copies of skeletons in several museums in North America, Europe, and Japan.

Large numbers of ceratopsid bones have been found in riverbeds. They probably came from entire herds that drowned while trying to cross flooded streams.

A *Triceratops* skeleton nearly 20 feet (6 m) long was displayed at the National Museum of Natural History in Washington for many years. It was

more than 8 feet (2.5 m) tall and was made of the bones of at least ten different dinosaurs. The skeleton was put together in 1905 using bones found by Hatcher in Wyoming.

During the 1990s, paleontologists noticed that the skeleton's back legs actually came from a duck-billed dinosaur. In October 1998, the skeleton was taken apart. The bones had been damaged by humidity. Recently, the skeleton was put back together. The skeleton now looks more accurate. However, the original bones are no longer displayed to avoid damaging them. All the bones in the new display are artificial.

A *Triceratops* skeleton from Montana is displayed at the Royal Tyrell Museum of Paleontology in Alberta, Canada.

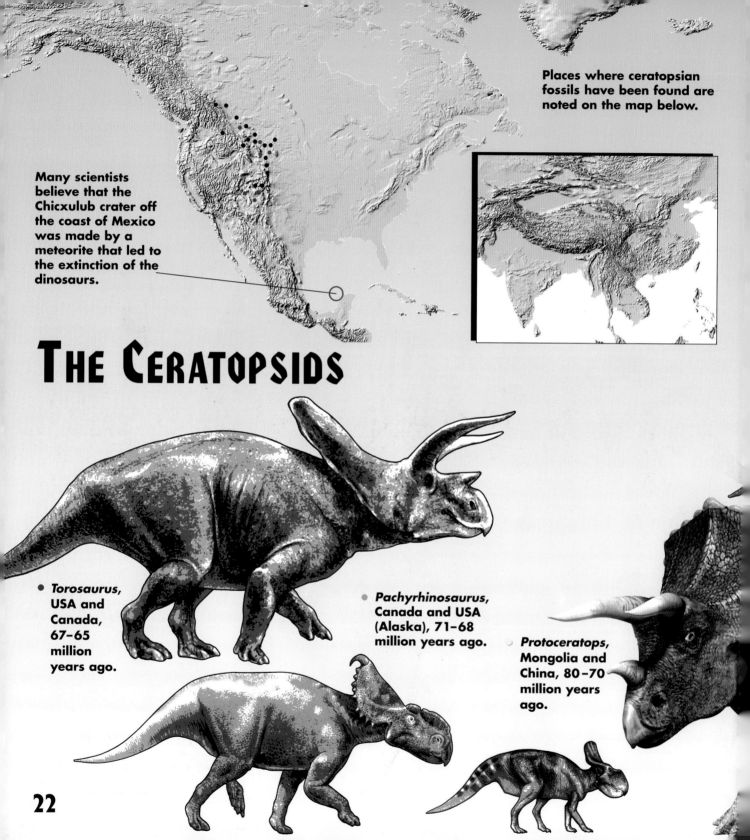

Places where ceratopsian fossils have been found are noted on the map below.

Many scientists believe that the Chicxulub crater off the coast of Mexico was made by a meteorite that led to the extinction of the dinosaurs.

THE CERATOPSIDS

- *Torosaurus, USA and Canada, 67–65 million years ago.*

- *Pachyrhinosaurus, Canada and USA (Alaska), 71–68 million years ago.*

- *Protoceratops, Mongolia and China, 80–70 million years ago.*

The ceratopsids, along with the duckbills, were the most common dinosaurs at the end of the Mesozoic era. They lived only in North America. Some paleontologists say there were two different species of *Triceratops*: *Triceratops horridus* and *Triceratops prorsus*. Others think the two types of *Triceratops* are simply the male and female of one species. Horned dinosaurs differ mainly in the size and number of horns they have, as well as the size and shape of the bony frill. The primitive *Protoceratops* did not have horns at all. *Styracosaurus* had six horns along the edge of its frill.

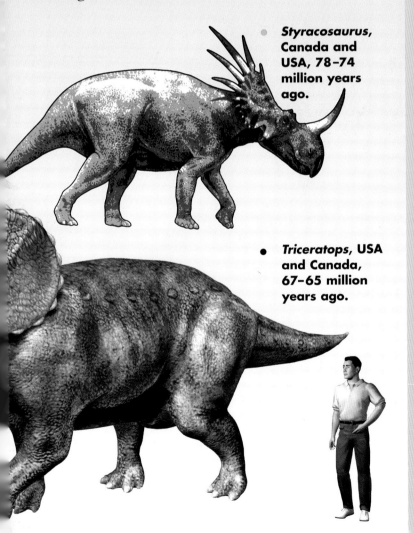

Styracosaurus, Canada and USA, 78–74 million years ago.

Triceratops, USA and Canada, 67–65 million years ago.

THE GREAT EXTINCTION

Sixty-five million years ago, when *Triceratops* was the most common large animal in North America, dinosaurs became extinct. This may have happened because a large meteorite struck Earth. A wide crater caused by a meteorite exactly 65 million years ago has been located along the coast of the Yucatán Peninsula in Mexico. The impact of the meteorite would have produced an enormous amount of dust. This dust would have stayed suspended in the atmosphere and blocked sunlight for a long time. A lack of sunlight would have caused a drastic drop of the earth's temperature and killed plants. The plant-eating dinosaurs would have died, starved and frozen. As a result, meat-eating dinosaurs would have had no prey and would also have starved.

Some scientists believe dinosaurs did not die out completely. They think that birds were feathered dinosaurs that survived the great extinction. That would make the present-day chicken and all of its feathered relatives descendants of the large dinosaurs.

THE EVOLUTION OF DINOSAURS

The oldest dinosaur fossils are 220–225 million years old and have been found mainly in South America. They have also been found in Africa, India, and North America. Dinosaurs probably evolved from small and nimble bipedal reptiles like the Triassic *Lagosuchus* of Argentina. Dinosaurs were able to rule the world because their legs were held directly under the body, like those of modern mammals. This made them faster and less clumsy than other reptiles.

Since 1887, dinosaurs have been divided into two groups based on the structure of their hips. Saurischian dinosaurs had hips shaped like those of modern lizards. Ornithischian dinosaurs had hips shaped like those of modern birds.

Triceratops is one of the Ornithischian dinosaurs, whose hip bones (inset) are shaped like those of modern birds.

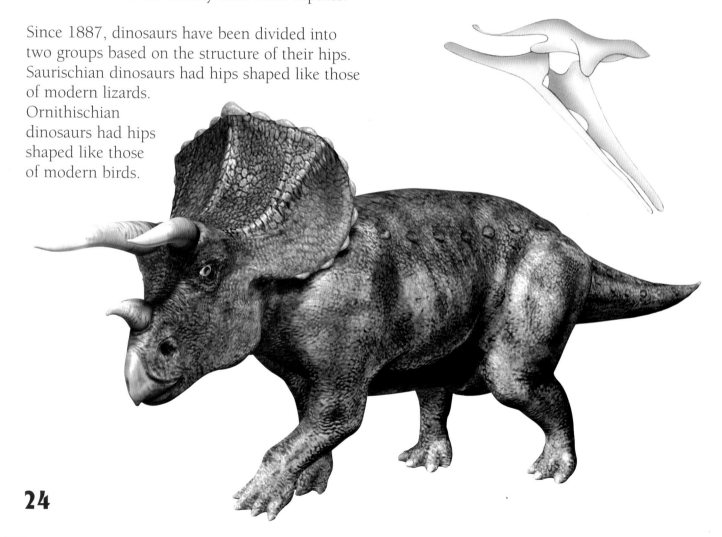

Tyrannosaurus is in the Saurischian group of dinosaurs, whose hip bones (inset) are shaped like those of modern lizards.

There are two main groups of saurischians. One group is sauropodomorphs. This group includes sauropods, such as *Brachiosaurus*. Sauropods ate plants and were quadrupedal, meaning they walked on four legs. The other group of saurischians, theropods, includes bipedal meat-eating predators. Some paleontologists believe birds are a branch of theropod dinosaurs.

Ornithischians are all plant eaters. They are divided into three groups. Thyreophorans include the quadrupedal stegosaurians, including *Stegosaurus*, and ankylosaurians, including *Ankylosaurus*. The other two groups are ornithopods, which includes *Edmontosaurus* and marginocephalians.

25

A DINOSAUR'S FAMILY TREE

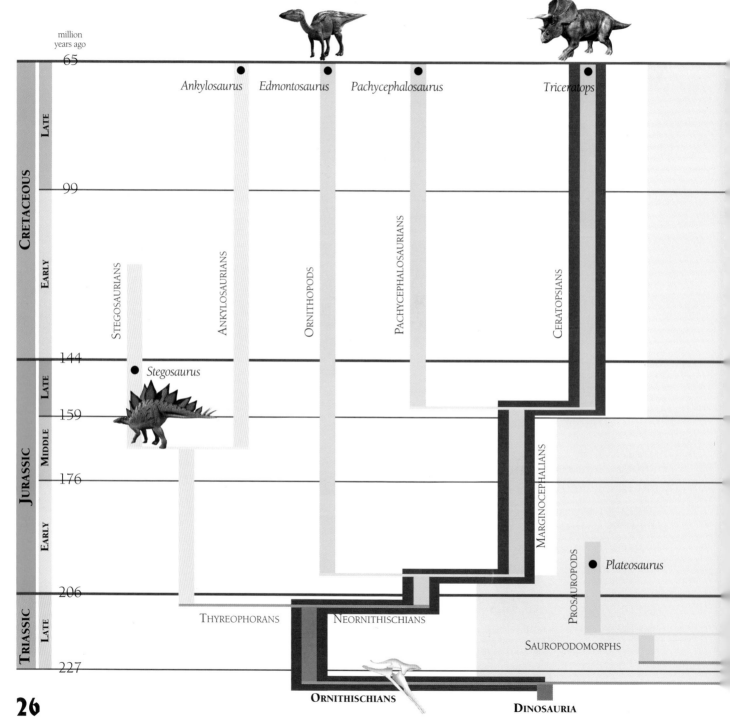

million
years ago

CRETACEOUS

LATE

EARLY

JURASSIC

LATE

MIDDLE

EARLY

TRIASSIC

LATE

65

99

144

159

176

206

227

Ankylosaurus   *Edmontosaurus*   *Pachycephalosaurus*   *Triceratops*

STEGOSAURIANS

ANKYLOSAURIANS

ORNITHOPODS

PACHYCEPHALOSAURIANS

CERATOPSIANS

Stegosaurus

MARGINOCEPHALIANS

PROSAUROPODS

Plateosaurus

THYREOPHORANS   NEORNITHISCHIANS

SAUROPODOMORPHS

ORNITHISCHIANS

DINOSAURIA

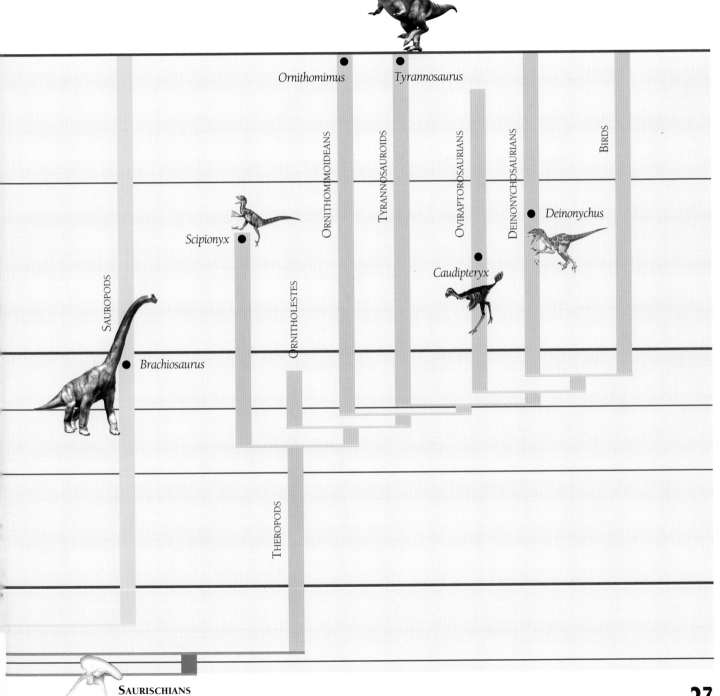

 ● Ornithomimus

● Tyrannosaurus

ORNITHOMIMOIDEANS

TYRANNOSAUROIDS

OVIRAPTOROSAURIANS

DEINONYCHOSAURIANS

BIRDS

● Deinonychus

Scipionyx ●

Caudipteryx ●

SAUROPODS

ORNITHOLESTES

● Brachiosaurus

THEROPODS

SAURISCHIANS

Glossary

Bipedal moving on two feet

Bone hard tissue made mainly of calcium phosphate

Caudal related to the tail

Cervical related to the neck

Cretaceous Period the period of geological time between 144 and 65 million years ago

Dorsal related to the back

Egg a large cell enclosed in a shell produced by reptiles and birds to reproduce themselves

Femur thigh bone

Fibula the outer of the two bones in the lower leg

Fossil a part of an organism of an earlier geologic age, such as a skeleton or leaf imprint, that has been preserved in the earth's crust

Jurassic Period the period of geological time between 206 and 144 million years ago

Mesozoic Era the period of geological time between 248 and 65 million years ago

Meteorite a piece of iron or rock that falls to Earth from space

Orbit opening in the skull surrounding the eye

Paleontologist a scientist who studies prehistoric life

Quadrupedal moving on four feet

Scapula shoulder blade

Skeleton the structure of an animal body, made up of bones

Skull the bones that form the cranium and the face

Tibia the shinbone

Triassic Period the period of geological time between 248 and 206 million years ago

Vertebrae the bones of the backbone

FOR MORE INFORMATION

Books

Paul M. Barrett, *National Geographic Dinosaurs*. Washington, DC: National Geographic Society, 2001.

Tim Haines, *Walking with Dinosaurs: A Natural History*. New York: Dorling Kindersley, 2000.

David Lambert, Darren Naish, and Elizabeth Wyse, *Dinosaur Encyclopedia: From Dinosaurs to the Dawn of Man*. New York: Dorling Kindersley, 2001.

Web Sites

The Cyberspace Museum of Natural History
www.cyberspacemuseum.com/dinohall.html
An online dinosaur museum that includes descriptions and illustrations.

Dinodata
www.dinodata.net
A site that includes detailed descriptions of fossils, illustrations, and news about dinosaur research and recent discoveries.

The Smithsonian National Museum of Natural History
www.nmnh.si.edu/paleo/dino
A virtual tour of the Smithsonian's National Museum of Natural History dinosaur exhibits.

ABOUT THE AUTHOR

Fabio Marco Dalla Vecchia is the curator of the Paleontological Museum of Monfalcone in Gorizia, Italy. He has participated in several paleontological field works in Italy and other countries and has directed paleontological excavations in Italy. He is the author of more than fifty scientific articles that have been published in national and international journals.

Index

Index

muscles, 8

neck, 8, 14

nests, 10

nostril, 10

ornithischians, 24–25, 26

ornithopods, 25

plant eaters, 14, 25

plants, 7, 12

predators, 10, 13, 16, 24

reptiles, 24

saurischians, 24–25, 27

skull, 14, 20

snout, 8

Stegosaurus, 7, 25

tail, 8

teeth, 16, 18

theropods, 25

toes, 18

Triassic period, 6

Triceratops, 7

  body, 8, 18–19

  size, 8

Tyrannosaurus, 7, 13, 16